I0714496

Copyright © Steven Cole and Eleni Dimitriou 2018
Published in England by AKAKIA Publications, 2018

STEVEN COLE - ELENI DIMITRIOU

Clumsy Mumsy
A FAMILY STORY

ISBN: 978-1-912322-46-6
Copyright © Steven Cole and Eleni Dimitriou 2018
CopyrightHouse.co.uk ID: 2093832

Cover Image:
Illustrator: Eleni Dimitriou
Book Design:
www.bluetreesstudio.co.uk

Àkakía
PUBLICATIONS

19 Ashmead, Chase Road,
N14 4QX, London, UK

T. 0044 207 1244 057
F. 0044 203 4325 030

www.akakia.net
publications@akakia.net

2018, London, UK

Marmalade Breakfast

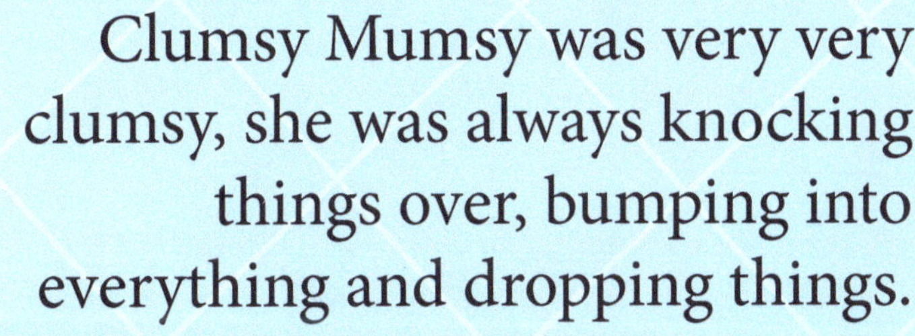

Clumsy Mumsy was very very clumsy, she was always knocking things over, bumping into everything and dropping things.

This day was no different.

It was 6 o'clock in the morning.

"Time to wake up" yawned Clumsy Mumsy but as
she stretched out her arms she accidentally hit the alarm
clock and sent it flying through the air crashing
down on Mr Mumsy's head.

4

"Ouch" yelled Mr Mumsy who was
woken up the same way **EVERY** morning.

She **WAS** clumsy, very clumsy.

"**What a beautiful day!**" said Clumsy Mumsy
"**I will pull the curtains and...**"
"**NOOOOOO, I'll do it!**" screamed Mr Mumsy,
but it was too late, Clumsy Mumsy pulled
the curtains far too hard and...

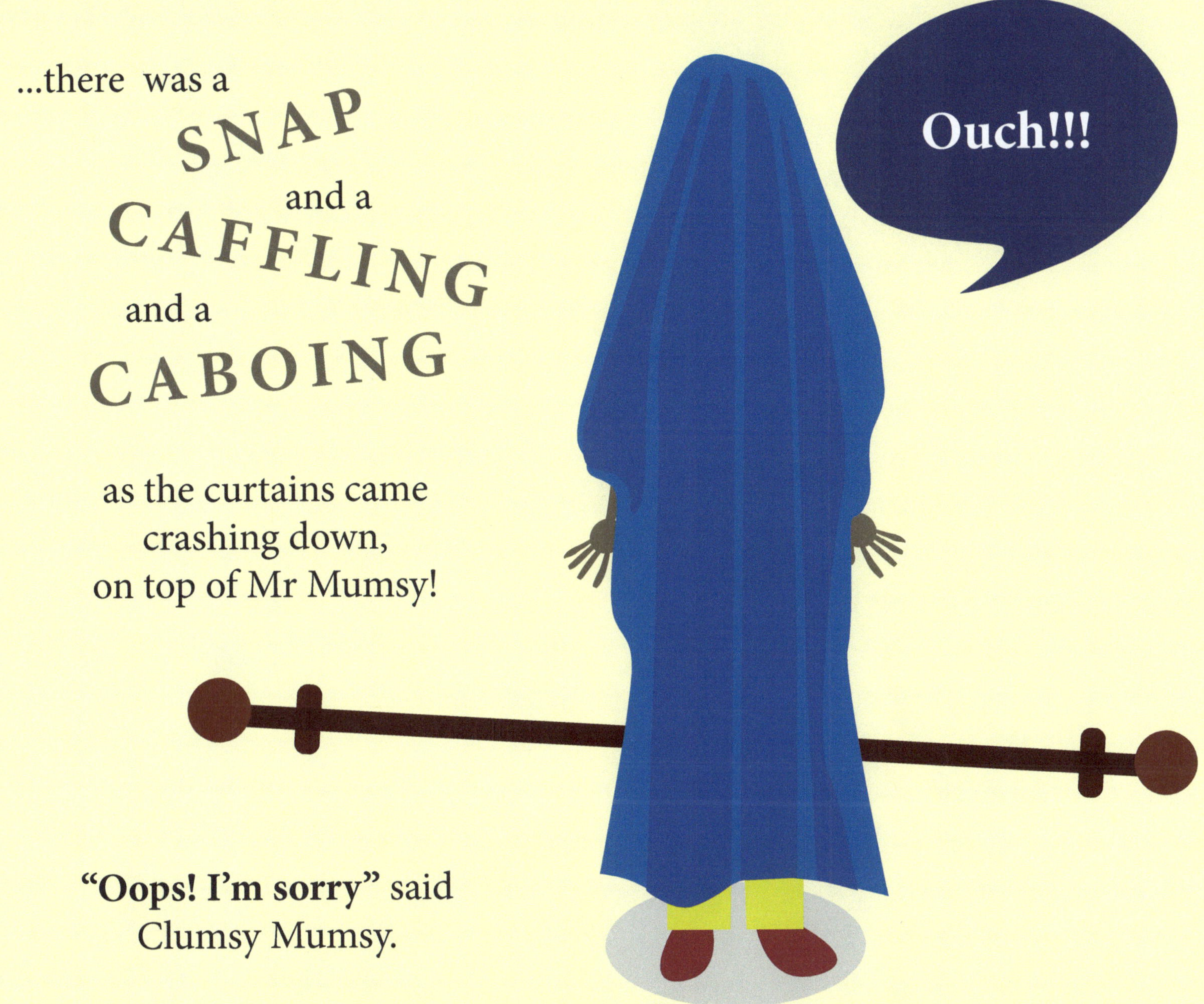

...there was a
SNAP
and a
CAFFLING
and a
CABOING

as the curtains came
crashing down,
on top of Mr Mumsy!

"Oops! I'm sorry" said
Clumsy Mumsy.

She **WAS** clumsy, very clumsy.

"It will soon be time for school,
I'd better wake the children up!" whispered Clumsy Mumsy
and she rushed out of the bedroom knocking
down the lamp, the flower vase and the goldfish bowl.

"NOOOOO!" yelled Mr Mumsy, "Let me do it!"

What Clumsy Mumsy didn't know was that the two children
were already up and stood behind their bedroom door.
"Don't worry, I can wake them!" said Clumsy Mumsy
and she slammed the bedroom door open...

... sending the two children flying through
the air and back into their beds.

"Come on you two" said Clumsy Mumsy,
**"You can't stay in bed all day!
I'm going to make you a lovely breakfast!"**

10

Both children looked worried.
Breakfast was a bit scary.

She **WAS** clumsy, very clumsy.

They would make up all kinds of excuses so
they wouldn't have to eat breakfast.

**"I don't have time for breakfast,
I promised to take next door's elephant
for a walk!"** said the little girl.

**"Oh yes, and I did say I would teach
the Giant Dragon how to play football"**
continued the little boy.

"Really! Well, that's very nice of you, but
I'm sure the dragon and the elephant can wait
until after breakfast.

And take those silly crash helmets off,
I don't know why you insist on wearing them
for breakfast, I really don't!"

"First of all, I'll need a big pot to make the porridge, a saucepan for the eggs and my favourite tea pot" said Clumsy.

Clumsy Mumsy loved making breakfast.

Mr Mumsy and the two children had no choice but
to sit there and wait. They knew what was going to happen,
you see, it was always the same, every morning.

Clumsy Mumsy went to open the pantry
door and tripped over the cat, which was
strange as they didn't have a cat!

She tripped over and went head first into
the pots and pans, some of which flew upwards
towards the kitchen ceiling, before coming down onto
Mr Mumsy and the two children's heads.

"**Sorry**" said Clumsy Mumsy, as she reached over to take a medium sized cooking pan from Mr Mumsy's rather sore head.

She **WAS** clumsy, very clumsy.

Then! Clumsy Mumsy turned away just for a second
accidentally pushing Mr Mumsy making him
fall back into the big green cabinet causing the cabinet
to come crashing down on top of the children.

"Children! Where are you? Are you ok?"
"We're under here" "We are under the cabinet"
said a voice from under the cabinet.

"Oops" said Clumsy Mumsy and she said that a lot.

She **WAS** clumsy,
very clumsy.

19

Clumsy Mumsy and Mr Mumsy tried to lift the cabinet,
but it was too heavy and Clumsy Mumsy dropped it on top of
Mr Mumsy's foot. There was an **"AAAAARGH"** and there
was an **"OW OW OW"**. Poor Mr Mumsy!
He screamed and yelled and he started to cry. He hopped
to the left, he hopped to the right, he hopped so high,

he got stuck in the light.

and HOPPED

"Oh nooooo!"
muttered Mr Mumsy.
The children giggled
"That can't be right?"

Clumsy Mumsy and the
children tried to help Mr Mumsy
and they all pulled and pulled
as hard as they could, but
the only thing to come down
was Mr Mumsy's trousers.

And, as always, Clumsy Mumsy had an idea!

**"I know what, we'll rub marmalade
around your head, then your head
will slip and slide out of the lampshade"**
said Clumsy Mumsy.

"Oh No! It's okay Dear, no need to help"
muttered a very distressed Mr Mumsy.
"I think I can get out myself", but it was too late…

Clumsy Mumsy got two big jars of marmalade and
told the children to start rubbing the marmalade all over
Mr Mumsy's head and on the inside of the lampshade.

"Okay Mumsy" giggled the children,
who both thought this was fun.
And to everyone's surprise!

"Its working! I'm nearly out" announced Mr Mumsy.
"If I can just…" "Don't worry, it'll be alright!" said Mrs Mumsy.
And with one more wiggle he was out of the light.

WIGGLED
WAGGLED
DODDLED
PIDDLED
"Maybe that wasn't a bad idea after all!" said Mr Mumsy.

25

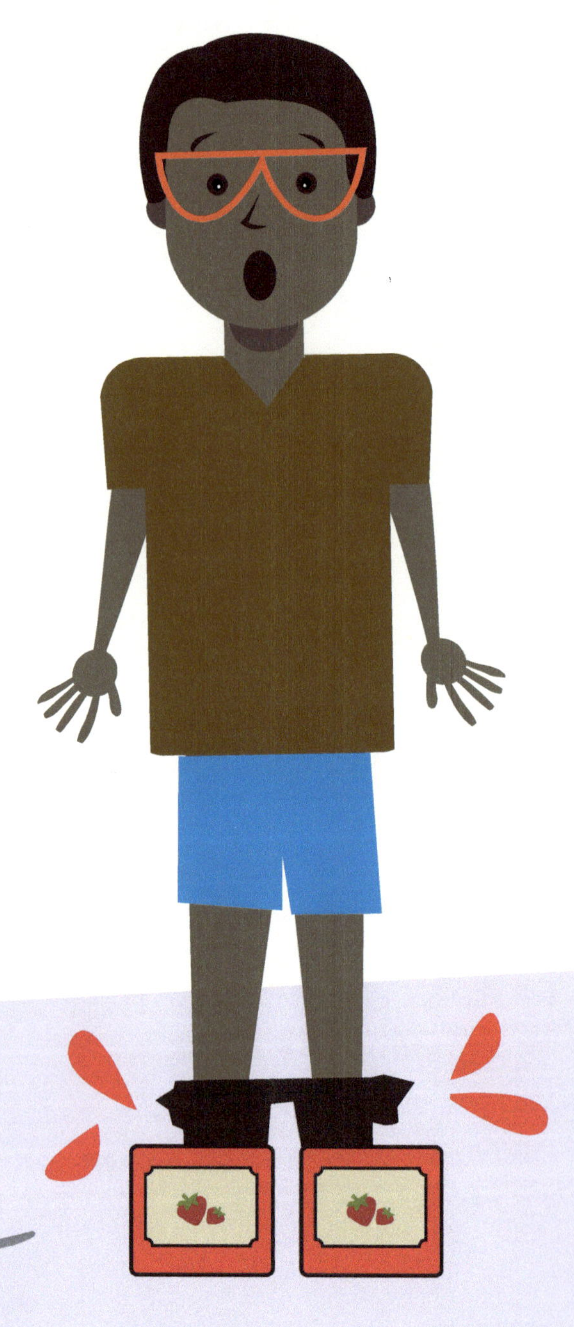

There was a shriek and
a frown, as Mr Mumsy came
hurtling down, landing firmly,
in the marmalade jars.
Mr Mumsy was not happy.
Well, you would be fed up
if you were stuck in jars of
marmalade, wouldn't you?

WOULDN'T YOU?

"Um, would you like toast with
your marmalade, Dear?"
said Clumsy Mumsy, who didn't
know what else to say.

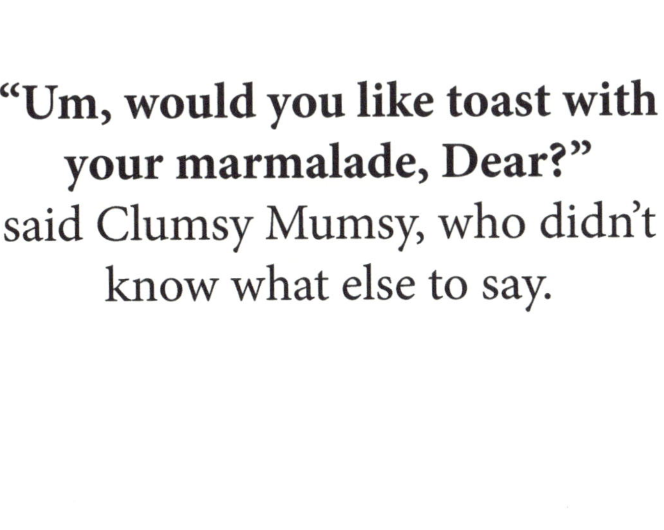

There was **SILENCE**…
nobody said a thing.

In the meantime, Clumsy Mumsy grabbed hold of the two jars
from Mr Mumsy's feet and pulled as hard as she could.

She pulled and she pulled, and with a **POPPITY POP POP** sound,
the two jars flew off of Mr Mumsy's feet and went flying through
the air, **SPINNING** and **TURNING**, **SPINNING** and **TURNING**, and
when she thought that was that - there was an almighty **SPLAT!!**

Landing instead on the two children's heads and now
it was **THEY** who were icky, it was **THEY** who were sticky!

"Oops, sorry", said Clumsy Mumsy.

WHAT A SIGHT IT WAS!

Mr Mumsy with his trousers around his ankles,
with a bump on his foot and a bump on his head,
two sorry looking children all icky and sticky with
a jar of marmalade on each head…
and funniest of all… it was only 10 minutes
since they got out of bed!

"Never mind" said Clumsy Mumsy.
It'll soon be time for dinner!
She WAS clumsy, very clumsy.

WHAT COULD POSSIBLY GO WRONG AT DINNER TIME?